The NIGHT BEFORE CHRISTMAS

The NIGHT BEFORE CHRISTMAS

CLEMENT C. MOORE

Photographs and drawings by

WILLIAM WEGMAN

Hyperion · New York

'TWAS

THE NIGHT BEFORE CHRISTMAS,

when all through the house

Not a creature was stirring,

not even a mouse;

The stockings were hung by the chimney with care,
In hopes that Saint Nicholas
　　　　　soon would be there;

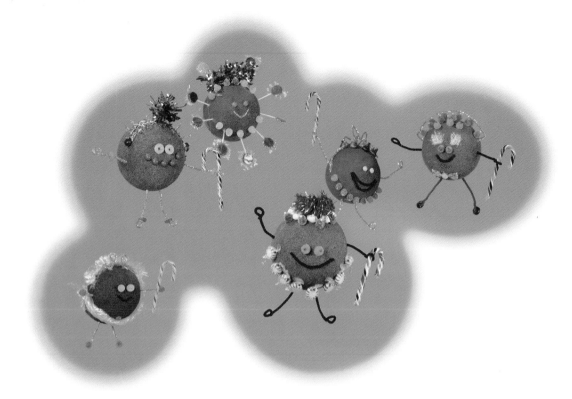

The children were nestled all snug in their beds,
While visions of sugarplums danced in their heads;

And Mama in her kerchief, and I in my cap,
Had just settled our brains
for a long winter's nap,

When out on the lawn there arose such a clatter,
I sprang from the bed to see what was the matter.

Away to the window I flew like a flash,
Tore open the shutters and threw up the sash.

The moon on the breast of the new-fallen snow
Gave the lustre of midday to objects below,

When, what to my wondering eyes should appear,
But a miniature sleigh, and eight tiny reindeer,

With a little old driver, so lively and quick,
I knew in a moment it must be Saint Nick.

More rapid than eagles his coursers they came,
And he whistled, and shouted,
and called them by name:

"Now, *Dasher!* now, *Dancer!* now,
Prancer and *Vixen!*
On, *Comet!* on, *Cupid!* on,
Donner and *Blitzen!*

To the top of the porch! to the top of the wall!
Now dash away! dash away! dash away all!"

As dry leaves that before the wild hurricane fly,
When they meet with an obstacle, mount to the sky,

So up to the housetop the coursers they flew,
With the sleigh full of toys,
and Saint Nicholas, too.

And then, in a twinkling, I heard on the roof
       The prancing and pawing
of each little hoof.

As I drew in my head, and was turning around,
       Down the chimney Saint Nicholas
          came with a bound.

He was dressed all in fur,
from his head to his foot,
And his clothes were all tarnished
with ashes and soot;

A bundle of toys he had flung on his back,
And he looked like
a peddler just opening his pack.

His eyes—how they twinkled! his dimples, how merry!
His cheeks were like roses, his nose like a cherry!

His droll little mouth was drawn up like a bow,
And the beard of his chin was as white as the snow;

The stump of a pipe he held tight in his teeth,
And the smoke it encircled his head like a wreath;

He had a broad face and a little round belly,
That shook when he laughed,
like a bowlful of jelly.

He was chubby and plump, a right jolly old elf,
And I laughed when I saw him, in spite of myself;

A wink of his eye and a twist of his head
Soon gave me to know
I had nothing to dread.

He spoke not a word, but went straight to his work,
And filled all the stockings;
then turned with a jerk,

And laying his finger aside of his nose,
And giving a nod,
up the chimney he rose;

He sprang to his sleigh, to his team gave a whistle,
And away they all flew like the down of a thistle.

But I heard him exclaim,
ere he drove out of sight,

HAPPY CHRISTMAS

TO

ALL

AND TO ALL

A GOOD NIGHT

The CAST

SANTA...Chip

FATHER (Narrator)...Chundo

MOTHER... Batty

CHILDREN... Batty, Bobbin, and Chip

REINDEER... Batty, Chip, Chundo, and Crooky

Batty

Chip

Bobbin

Crooky

Chundo

Bill

The CREW

Erick Matt Heather Andrea Jason Pam

ACKNOWLEDGMENTS

With thanks to Andrea Beeman and Jason Burch; Jen Allison, Susan Bransfield, Katherine Brown Tegen, Christine Burgin,

Mike Cirelli, Mary Dinaburg, Fotocare, Matt Garton, Charles Goldfine, Peggy Jordan, Azan Kung, Dave McMillan,

Marion Maloney, Erick Michaud, Heather Murray, Picture Ray Studio, Saks Fifth Avenue, Ken Smart,

Mr. and Mrs. Samuel C.J. Spivey, Studio One, Gary Tooth, and Pam Wegman.

Printed in Singapore

This book is set in Poetica & Mrs. Eaves.

Design by Empire Design Studio, NYC

First edition

1 3 5 7 9 10 8 6 4 2

Library of Congress Cataloging-in-Publication Data

Moore, Clement Clarke, 1779–1863.

The night before Christmas / Clement C. Moore ; photographs and drawings by William Wegman.— 1st ed.

p. cm.

Summary: The familiar Christmas poem is illustrated with photographs of dogs.

ISBN 0-7868-0608-7 (trade)

1. Santa Claus—Juvenile poetry. 2. Christmas—Juvenile poetry. 3. Children's poetry,

American. [1. Santa Claus—Poetry. 2. Christmas—Poetry. 3. American poetry.

4. Narrative poetry.] I. Wegman, William, ill. II. Title.

PS2429.M5 N5   2000

811'.2—dc21

00-38482

Visit www.hyperionchildrensbooks.com